Pet to School Day

Published by
Evans Brothers Limited
2A Portman Mansions
Chiltern St
London W1U 6NR

Reprinted 2007

British Library Cataloguing in Publication Data

Robinson, Hilary, 1962-
         Pet to school day. - (Zig zags)
         1. Children's stories - Pictorial works
         I. Title
         823.9'14 [J]

ISBN 0 237 52773 1
13-digit ISBN (from 1 Jan 2007) 978 0 237 52773 0

Printed in China by WKT Company Limited

Series Editor: Nick Turpin
Design: Robert Walster
Production: Jenny Mulvanny
Series Consultant: Gill Matthews

ZIG ZAG

Pet to School Day

by Hilary Robinson

illustrated by Tim Archbold

Evans

"Today is pet day,"
said Mr Spink.

"Where's your pet, sir?"

"At home. He's too wild."

"Is he a bull?"

"Is he an elephant?"

"No," said Mr Spink.
"My pet is a…

...dinosaur!"

14

"Have you had him for
thousands of years?"

"I caught him on Sunday.
He wears a red collar, eats
trees and drinks from the bath."

"Where can you catch
dinosaurs?"
"In a dinosaur park."

18

"How?"
"With a dinosaur net,"
replied Mr Spink.

20

"Can anyone do that?"

"Only with a permit," said
Mr Spink.
"When you catch a dinosaur
you get a badge like mine."

"How can you get a permit?"
asked James.

"You have to show that you are a brave dinosaur warrior," said Mr Spink.

"You're not!"

"How do you know I'm not?"
asked Mr Spink.

"Because you're scared of
spiders and," said James,
"to prove it, this is…

Max!"

Why not try reading another ZigZag book?

Dinosaur Planet   ISBN 0 237 52793 6
by David Orme and Fabiano Fiorin

Tall Tilly   ISBN 0 237 52794 4
by Jillian Powell and Tim Archbold

Batty Betty's Spells   ISBN 0 237 52795 2
by Hilary Robinson and Belinda Worsley

The Thirsty Moose   ISBN 0 237 52792 8
by David Orme and Mike Gordon

The Clumsy Cow   ISBN 0 237 52790 1
by Julia Moffatt and Lisa Williams

Open Wide!   ISBN 0 237 52791 X
by Julia Moffatt and Anni Axworthy

Too Small   ISBN 0 237 52777 4
by Kay Woodward and Deborah van de Leijgraaf

I Wish I Was An Alien   ISBN 0 237 52776 6
by Vivian French and Lisa Williams

The Disappearing Cheese   ISBN 0 237 52775 8
by Paul Harrison and Ruth Rivers

Terry the Flying Turtle   ISBN 0 237 52774 X
by Anna Wilson and Mike Gordon

Pet To School Day   ISBN 0 237 52773 1
by Hilary Robinson and Tim Archbold

The Cat in the Coat   ISBN 0 237 52772 3
by Vivian French and Alison Bartlett